# The Wild Boy

BASED ON THE TRUE STORY OF THE WILD BOY OF AVEYRON

## MORDICAI GERSTEIN

*A Sunburst Book* · *Farrar, Straus and Giroux*

Copyright © 1998 by Mordicai Gerstein
All rights reserved
Distributed in Canada by Douglas & McIntyre Ltd.
Printed in Singapore
First edition, 1998
Sunburst edition, 2002
3 5 7 9 10 8 6 4

Library of Congress Cataloging-in-Publication Data
Gerstein, Mordicai.
    The wild boy / Mordicai Gerstein. — 1st ed.
        p.   cm.
    "Based on the true story of the Wild Boy of Aveyron."
    "Frances Foster books."
    Summary: Relates the story of a boy who grew up like a wild animal
in the forests of France and was later captured and studied by doctors in
Paris, but never became completely civilized.
    ISBN-13: 978-0-374-48396-8 (pbk.)
    ISBN-10: 0-374-48396-5 (pbk.)
    1. Wild Boy of Aveyron—Juvenile literature.   2. Feral children—
Juvenile literature.   [1. Wild Boy of Aveyron.   2. Feral children.]
I. Title.
GN372.G47   1998
155.45´67—dc21

                                                          97-37246

For my daughter, Risa, my sons, Jesse and Aram,
my grandchildren, Daisy and Hugh, and
for the Wild Child in everyone,
myself included

ONCE THERE WAS A BOY who lived in the
mountain forests of southern France.

He lived completely alone, without mother, father, or friends. He didn't know what a mother or father was. He was naked. He didn't know what clothes were. He didn't know he was a boy, or even a person. He didn't know what people were.

He was completely wild.

He knew how to live in the wild woods. He knew which plants, berries, and roots would nourish him. He was always hungry.

He knew how to survive the harsh winters, the long, icy nights. He didn't seem to feel the cold.

No one but the animals knew he lived there. He
didn't talk to them because he didn't know what
talking was. He didn't befriend them because he didn't
know what friends were. Sometimes the fiercer
animals attacked him. He had to fight. His body was
covered with scars.

He loved the wind.

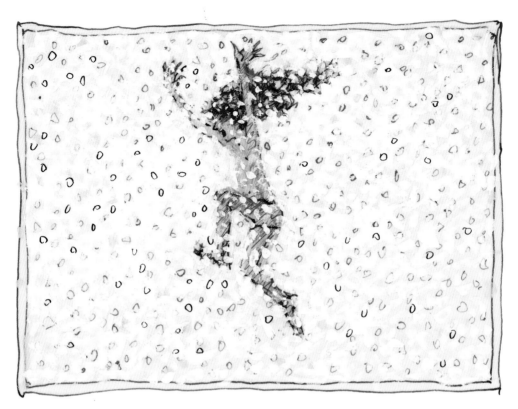

He loved the snow.
He loved the full moon.

He loved the icy water from the mountain streams
and drank with his chin touching the mossy rocks.
He was completely wild.

One gray winter morning, three men saw him.
They were hunting. At first they thought he was some
kind of animal. Then they weren't sure.

They chased him through the woods.

He tried to escape up a tree, but they caught him.

They brought him to a town, and the people stared
at him. They had never seen a wild boy. He looked at
the people. He didn't know what they were.

"He must have had parents," they said. But no one
knew who they might be, or how he came to live in
the wild woods.

He didn't know, either.

The town officials took charge of him. They spoke
to him, but he didn't listen. He didn't know what
words were.

"He's deaf and mute," they said.

He tried to run back to the mountains, but they caught him and put him on a leash. When they first put clothes on him, he tore them off. They gave him a bed, but he wouldn't sleep in it. All he would eat was walnuts, and baked potatoes still smoldering from the fire.

He cared only for food and freedom.

Word was sent to Paris:

"A Wild Boy Has Been Captured!"

It was in all the newspapers. They printed

drawings that showed him with claws, fur, and a tail.

Scientists and scholars wanted to study him.

He was taken to Paris, over three hundred miles
from his mountains, by coach. As the coach clattered
into the city, he didn't even look out the windows. The
grand buildings and swarms of people didn't interest
him. The forest was the only place he knew, and Paris
wasn't a forest.

He was taken to the Institute for Deaf-Mutes, to be examined and tested. They shouted at him and fired pistols near his ear. He didn't even blink. But they found he wasn't deaf. He turned his head when a walnut was cracked in the next room. He loved walnuts.

He would not eat bread, meat, or sweets, but only nuts, boiled beans, and potatoes baked in the coals. He plucked them from the fire and ate them burning-hot.

"He seems to feel no pain!" marveled the experts. They showed him toys and books; they rang bells and played music; they poked him and pinched him. They couldn't get his attention. His mind was in the woods. His ears listened for wind and wolves.

He cared only for food and freedom.

After weeks of tests and examinations, the experts made an announcement.

"The boy's behavior," they said, "places him below all animals, wild or domestic. He is hopeless."

Then they lost interest in him.

Except for one man.

Jean-Marc Itard was a young doctor at the Institute. He was quiet and thoughtful. He saw the boy ignored and uncared for, growing wilder than ever.

Itard watched as the boy sat quietly by the lily pond and gazed into the water for hours. The boy's eyes were deep and sad. From time to time he gently scattered a handful of dry leaves onto the surface of the water, and watched them float away.

Dr. Itard saw a boy who had never been held or sung to or played with. He saw a child who had never learned to be a child.

He decided to take the boy home and care for him. "I will be your teacher," the doctor said to him.

The doctor's housekeeper, Madame Guérin, a kind,
motherly woman, tried to hug the boy when he
arrived, but he grabbed her hand and sniffed it all
over. He sniffed everything.

"What's his name?" asked Madame Guérin, laughing.

"He's never been given one," said the doctor, "but
I've noticed that he seems to like the sound 'Oh.' His
name should have that sound in it."

"How about VicTOR?" asked Madame Guérin.

The boy looked at her.

"Victor!" said the doctor. "I believe it will suit him."

They took Victor for long runs in the country. He
went wild with joy. They made him comfortable in his
own room, and gave him plenty of his favorite foods.

One morning, it snowed. The doctor looked out
and was amazed to see Victor, naked and laughing,
rolling in the snow. He hugged it to his body and
stuffed his mouth with it.

"His skin," the doctor explained to Madame Guérin, "has never learned the difference between hot and cold, rough and smooth. We have to teach him to feel."

They gave Victor hot baths and massaged his scarred body.

Victor began to feel the warmth of the water and the care in their hands. After a few weeks, he wouldn't get into the water if it was too cold.

On chilly mornings, he began to dress himself.

He learned to use a spoon instead of his hands to take potatoes out of boiling water, or the fire.

He came to love the feel of Madame Guérin's velvet dress.

But Victor's gaze still flitted from one thing to another. Only food got his full attention.

The doctor had an idea: he showed Victor a walnut, then put it under a cup and mixed it up among other cups.

Victor watched carefully and immediately turned over the right cup. The doctor hid the nut again and again, and Victor laughed and found it every time.

Even when the doctor replaced the walnut with a ball, Victor always found it on his first try.

"Bravo, Victor!" cried the doctor. "You've learned to pay attention, and you've learned to *play*!"

Day after day, the doctor worked hard with Victor, trying to teach him to speak. Months passed, but Victor seemed unable to learn. The doctor grew discouraged, and finally impatient.

"What's the use?" he shouted one day. "Go back to the forest, Victor! Live like an animal!"

He saw Victor's eyes fill with pain and then tears.
Never before had the doctor seen him weep. He
hugged Victor and rocked him as the boy wailed and
sobbed and the tears ran down his face.

"Forgive me, Victor. You are not an animal. You
are a boy. A wonderful boy."

He will never learn to speak, thought the doctor
sadly. He was alone in the silent woods too long. But
he *has* learned to have feelings, and they can be hurt.

Victor learned to recognize different colors and shapes. Then he learned to recognize letters.

The doctor made an alphabet of cut-out letters, and Victor learned to spell *lait,* the French word for milk. He always took those letters with him when they went to a restaurant, and used them to order milk for himself.

Victor learned to read more words and to connect them to things and ideas. He learned to write the words he knew.

One sweet spring morning, Victor woke and, without thinking, ran off to find the woods. He became lost in the suburbs of Paris and spent the night hiding in a park till the police found him.

When Madame Guérin came for him, he hugged and kissed her, and wept with joy.

I believe he loves Madame Guérin more than he loves me, the doctor said wistfully to himself. That's natural, I suppose, in a boy.

Victor loved setting the table, or anything else he could do to be helpful.

Sawing firewood filled him with happiness and pride. He loved the fragrant wood and the sound of the saw. He was skillful at feeding and tending the fires.

When he solved a difficult problem in his studies, or the doctor praised him, he beamed with pleasure.

He loved order and straightened his room every day.

He combed his hair and polished his shoes.

He wasn't wild anymore.

But he did remain silent, and could never tell of his wild life. And something of the wild was always in him.

He loved pure icy water and loved to drink it slowly while looking out the window at the sky and the trees.

The sound of a rising wind, or the sight of whirling snowflakes or the sun bursting from behind a cloud, still made him tremble with excitement and a wild joy.

And every evening, when the doctor sat on Victor's bed, Victor took the doctor's hand and covered his own eyes and forehead with it and held it there, without moving, for a long while.

They sat like this for an hour sometimes, and then the doctor would kiss him and say good night.

And if the doctor looked back in on him when the
moon was full, Victor was always gazing up into it,
perfectly still, bathed in silver light.

I wonder what he sees, thought the doctor.

I wonder what he feels.

I wonder . . .

The boy known as Victor, the wild child of Aveyron, was captured in the town of Saint-Sernin in the Aveyron district of southern France on January 8, 1800. After being studied by a local naturalist, he was sent to Paris for further study by scientists there. He arrived in Paris on August 6, just a few months after Napoleon Bonaparte took control of the French republic. Almost all the experts declared Victor hopelessly retarded, but a twenty-six-year-old doctor, Jean-Marc-Gaspard Itard, believed Victor's animal-like behavior and inability to speak were the result of his having lived alone for years in the wild. Itard worked with Victor for six years, and while much progress was made, Victor never learned to speak.

Dr. Itard wrote two reports on his work with the boy and became world famous. Many of the teaching methods he devised are now used in special education, and Maria Montessori based much of her work on Itard's reports.

Madame Guérin continued to care for Victor in a small house in Paris until he died in 1828 at about the age of forty. His origins are still a mystery.